UNFAITHFUL

SUSAN M BAER

Find out more about Susan M. Baer and her upcoming books online at
www.susanbaerauthor.com

Unfaithful

1

Judgment Day

Jeremy felt his head press heavily into the cushion as he struggled to stay awake. The fabric held tight to his skin and pulled the corner of his mouth back at an odd angle. He had sunk deep into the couch and only his right eye could still see the blurred figure across from him. His entire body had turned to lead and his limbs refused to move. The thought that he had become one with the furniture amused him, but the smile wouldn't come to his face and the laughter stayed trapped in his heart.

He blinked slowly but only his right eye closed. The fibers in the paisley material tangled with the lashes on his left and held the eyelid open. That was so bizarre. At least he was pretty sure it was, unless that was what happened when you drank too much. He wouldn't know. He had never been this drunk before.

He thought back to his first sip of bourbon and realized he probably should have passed on the nightcap. But the guilt of his betrayal had manifested into agonizing physical symptoms, and the multiple doses of ibuprofen had had no effect on the pain. So he had hoped the alcohol would have helped him relax. Instead, it had turned out to be just one more poor decision to add to his growing list of regrets.

His wife had agreed to let him stop by the house this morning to pick up the last of his boxes. She had already left for work so he had decided to check the bedroom for evidence of the man he had suspected she had been sleeping with. He had found her diary sitting on the nightstand and had flipped through the pages looking for the bastard's name. Instead, each entry had been about him, and her words had shredded his heart. Everything he had believed about the destruction of their marriage had been wrong, and everything he had done because of his misconceptions had only made things worse. By the time he had backed his car out of the driveway, he had cancelled his meetings for the day. He had something more important to do.

He had driven around and visited all the places that had been special to him and his wife. One by one the memories had retold the love story he and his wife had written since the moment they had met. By five o'clock, he was on his way home to Genevieve and he had finally seen his life as clearly as his wife had all along. There was only one way to fix the disaster his life had become. He had to tell Genevieve it was over. He was going back to his wife.

He tried to focus his vision on Genevieve, but his eyes defied the command to move. She was barely visible as her dark shape moved closer to him. Her face became clearer when she knelt in front of him and kissed his forehead. He saw her take hold of his hand, but he felt nothing. That was definitely unsettling, and then it got worse. A disturbing heaviness squeezed his heart an instant before he rushed toward the ceiling.

The space around him became bright and he was standing in a field of lush grass. In front of him, he could see a vision of his lifeless body resting on the couch he and Genevieve had bought just a month ago. She was kneeling on the floor and sobbing desperately as she clutched his head to her breast.

"Come, Jeremy," a gentle voice said. "It is time."

He turned around and an angel stood in the midst of the most beautiful landscape he had ever seen. The sun was bright in the sky, yet he had no need to squint. The light penetrated his soul and filled him with a peace so beyond words that he knew his smile would never fade. A gentle breeze caressed the limbs of the trees as they hung low with the weight of gorgeous blossoms and vibrant leaves. Birds of every color soared on the wind currents and sang like angels. The sound of gentle waves complimented their voices and he turned to see an endless horizon of crystal blue water.

"This is heaven," Jeremy said. "Why am I here?"

"Actually, you are not in heaven. Yet." The angel touched his shoulder. "This is the island of Repose."

"Repose?"

"Yes." The angel led him to the path at the edge of the trees. "It is here you will receive your judgment."

Jeremy looked down the trail and a trace of dread crept into his heart. He was not ready for this. He needed more time.

"My judgment?" he whispered.

"Do not be afraid."

"But I am too young to die." He shook his head. "I am healthy. There-there is nothing wrong with me."

"Your time has come. God has called you home."

"No. I am not worthy. I have done some terrible things."

"Still your thoughts. You have nothing to fear. You would not be here if you were not already destined for paradise."

"How can that be?" Jeremy hesitated. "I didn't make things right."

"Come." The angel smiled and motioned for him to follow the path in front of him. "He is waiting for you."

Jeremy looked forward and the space before him became immense. The path was now behind him and he stood at the edge of a clearing. Light filled every crevice and peace surrounded him. Winged men in simple, yet beautiful, robes sat in a circle around the Savior. Jesus looked at him and time stood still. The Son of God smiled and Jeremy felt like a child on Christmas morning. Joy became the only emotion he could feel and he could find no words worthy of speaking in the moment.

"I have claimed you before my Father," Jesus said, "and He is pleased. Come forward and listen to His judgement."

Jeremy stepped into the circle and sat on a bench of fragrant lilies. Jesus stood and faded from his view before the angels addressed him. One by one, they showed him events in his life. Some were significant and memorable while others he had forgotten about completely. Each one detailed an important crossroad in his life that had changed the direction of his path.

Despite his fear, the angels had assured him God was pleased. Yet before he could enter paradise, he must first acknowledge his final sin and desire forgiveness for his betrayal.

2

Purgatory

Robert Castle stood on the porch of DeLancey Manor with Beauty sitting at his heel. George and the guardians were gone, and darkness covered Cedar Rock Mountain once again. He pulled his pocket watch from the vest pouch of his suit and looked at the time. He furrowed his eyebrows and studied the old timepiece. The hands were moving, it was working, but...

"Eleven fifteen?" he whispered. "That can't be right. When George and I left for Repose it was already after midnight."

"Excuse me, Master Robert," a man at the bottom of the porch stairs said, "I was told you could help me."

Robert looked at the man. He was dressed in a dark blue suit with a white shirt and a red tie. His light brown hair was clean cut and styled to hide the few gray strands he had found several years ago, and his face was freshly shaven. He looked every bit the businessman he had always been. The only thing missing was the leather briefcase he had never left home without.

Headlights moved closer along the drive and Robert watched Father Kelly park his car near the side of the house. He had come to help. In the darkness, Robert heard the wind rustle the leaves of the trees that lined the eastern shore of the lake, and he knew an angel was on his way. He scanned the darkness for a glimpse of him, but no one had appeared yet. He exhaled. He wasn't sure how he knew all these things, but he was certain his facts were accurate.

"Master Robert," the man said again, "can you hear me?"

"Yes, Mr. Greene," Robert said. "I can hear you."

Robert took one step down and stopped. He knew this man, but he didn't know how. He had never met him, yet he knew very specific details about him. His name was Jeremy Greene and he was forty-six years old. He had a beautiful wife, Alice, and an equally beautiful twenty-three-year-old daughter, Jessica. He was a hard worker and had moved quickly up the corporate ladder at Readimed

Equipment. In fact, he was on the short list of candidates for the VP of Sales and Marketing... or well, he had been. Mr. Greene was deceased.

A gust of wind rushed past Robert and a tall and slender winged man landed swiftly next to Beauty. The angel towered over the wolf. His wings furled against his body and dissolved into his clothing. He bowed his head to Robert then gave Beauty a scratch behind her ear as his being subsided to a more humanly stature. Still, Robert guessed he was about seven feet tall.

"Master Robert," he said, "please forgive my intrusion into your thoughts."

"Excuse me?" Robert said.

"I had hoped to speak to you in a more traditional manner. However, Mr. Greene is quite anxious to speak with you, so I sent the basics ahead of my arrival."

"I don't understand."

"I gave you the necessary information on your journey back from Repose." The angel descended a step and stood next to Robert. "The Master of the house must be kept informed of all matters. Therefore, you needed to know who was waiting for you."

Robert watched Fr. Kelly greet Mr. Greene. The clergyman was the pastor of St. James Church in Crescent Valley. Robert remembered him from his childhood years. The pastor gave him a nod of recognition then guided Jeremy away from the house. They headed toward the lake and disappeared into the darkness.

"So, you are the Angel of Death." Robert kept his eyes on the spot where the men had vanished.

"I prefer Nathaniel if you don't mind," he said. "That title is grievously misunderstood by your kind."

"I'm sorry." Robert turned to face him. "I meant no offense."

"Neither does the bachelor who calls his son a bastard."

Beauty heeled to Robert's side and raised her muzzle to his chest. He caressed her side before she bared her teeth to Nathaniel and positioned herself between the two.

Nathaniel bowed his head to her and clasped his hands behind his back before he spoke again.

"I apologize for my insolent tone, Master Robert. It was not intended for you."

"Thank you," Robert said.

Beauty growled and yipped, then poked her muzzle hard into Nathaniel's gut. The angel placed his hand over his heart and bowed his head to her.

"My apologies to you as well, my lady. It shall not happen again."

Robert suppressed his grin. Apparently, Beauty was in charge on this mountain.

"You are not what I expected," Robert said.

"I am not?"

"No. I thought you would look... different."

"Different how?" Nathaniel cocked his head.

"I didn't picture you in a suit."

"I always wear a suit when I am conducting business on this mountain." He rocked back on his heels. "Otherwise, I wear something more comfortable."

"When do you wear your black robe?"

"I have never worn a black robe, nor will I ever." He hooded his gaze.

"But all the images of you have you in a black hooded robe with a sickle. I had assumed someone had to have seen you that way to record the image."

"It is called a scythe." Nathaniel scowled. "And I can thank Malachi for that asinine image."

"Malachi?"

"My brother."

"Your brother." Robert raised his eyebrows. "I didn't know the angel-of what you do-had any family."

"Families in our world are different than yours. Malachi and I are not brothers because we are from one flesh. We are brothers because we were forged from one spirit to carry out the same purpose."

"So, your brother is the one who kills people."

"Tell me you do not seriously believe the rubbish you just uttered."

Beauty growled low in her throat.

"Yes, my lady," Nathaniel said to Beauty. "I am trying." He exhaled and looked at Robert. "Neither my brother nor I are able to take a life prematurely. That power is reserved for mortals."

"I thought God was the only One who could determine the end of our lives."

"Our Father knows all. Nothing escapes His awareness. However, a mortal's free will determines their release from the flesh."

"What do you mean?"

"It is quite simple, really, and it is one of the greatest perils of free will. Every decision a mortal makes plays a part in their journey toward death, including those decisions that place them at the mercy of another's free will."

"I don't understand."

"Look at what you know about Mr. Greene and you will find the answer."

Robert looked toward the lake and saw Fr. Kelly and Jeremy standing under the flood light at the end of the dock. He searched the information Nathaniel had given him and focused on Jeremy's last day. He had died unexpectedly. A perfectly healthy man closed his eyes and quietly passed from this world.

"Genevieve," Robert said. "His mistress murdered him."

"Precisely." Nathaniel sat on the top step next to Beauty and leaned his elbows on his knees. "Jeremy became involved with Miss Genevieve Carter of his own free will. Together, the two created the moment when Genevieve, a mere mortal woman, crushed a lethal dose of pills into a powder and dissolved the substance into a glass of bourbon. Then she gave it to her lover and watched him drift away from her world as his mortal flesh was robbed of life, one organ at a time." He paused. "The Lord did not take his life. Mr. Greene's mistress did."

Robert sat next to Beauty and stroked her side as he replayed the scene. Jeremy had grown drowsy faster than he had expected, but he had convinced himself he was simply more tired than he had realized. His vision had blurred and his chest had ached with the labored beats of his heart, so he had closed his eyes to take a deep breath, and collapsed onto the couch.

When the air had left Jeremy's lungs for the final time, Genevieve had closed her eyes to let the hot tears flow down her cheeks. She had regretted her sin even before his spirit was gone.

"Does Jeremy know what she did?" Robert said.

"Yes. He was shown the details of his death, including the last hour while his spirit was leaving the flesh."

"And he saw her crying as she held his cold hand?"

"Yes."

"Does he understand why she did it?"

Robert looked at the lost soul sitting on the end of the dock with his head in his hands and felt pity for him.

"No." Nathaniel sighed. "That is why he is still here."

3

More Than a Groundskeeper

Robert sat in the window seat in his dining room and scrolled through his emails. Working from home had its perks, but it also had its drawbacks. The amount of emails he normally got from his staff had quadrupled. Since the only cell signal he could get on this mountain was at the dock, he had instructed them to email him instead. He had not realized how many times a day he spoke to each of them. The sheer volume of questions was depressing. Maybe he needed to be a little less accessible to everyone and limit his communications to a few senior employees. In the meantime, he had made a folder for each person and sorted the emails before he opened them.

He scanned each folder for subjects that looked like priorities while he tossed around some ideas on how to deal with the soul still standing at the edge of the lake. Jeremy had been left to work through some thoughts Fr. Kelly had discussed with him. That was three days ago. Nathaniel had told Robert he would know when the time was right to talk to Jeremy, but Robert was afraid he had missed his cue while he was learning the ropes in this whole "Master of the Manor" thing.

Since the morning after his initiation, Cedar Rock had become populated with thousands of souls. They traveled through purgatory at their own paces with some staying only minutes, and all of them talking their way through their penance. Whether they were discussing their journeys with other souls or with themselves, every story Robert had heard had stayed in the forefront of his thoughts. After only an hour, he had felt like he was losing himself in an endless flood of voices. That was when Eleanor had brought him a bowl of fresh raspberries and had shown him how to use the diary.

The master's diary was a godsend. As soon as he recorded a soul's name, their story left his mind, and he was free of the cluttering thoughts. When the souls passed by too quickly, he simply had to touch the quill to the page and their names appeared on the divine parchment, while their stories and voices vanished from his head. But they were not gone forever. If he wanted to revisit a soul's journey, he simply had to touch their name with his fingertips and their story replayed in his mind.

His time with Eleanor was shorter than he had hoped. It had been three days since he had been able to visit with someone who didn't need his help. But she was from the other world, and her time spent in his was limited. He had just resigned himself to being alone when he had looked up from the diary and had seen Shamus standing next to the mantle with two mugs of raspberry schnapps in his fists.

After an hour or so of reminiscing about his favorite tales as the master, Shamus had taught Robert the fine art of seeing a single soul more clearly than the thousands of others passing through. Conveniently enough, when the images faded from his sight, the voices faded from his ears.

Shamus had claimed it was a simple exercise of mind over matter, but Robert was certain the schnapps had a little something to do with it. There was no denying it had a definite effect on him, although it was nothing like what he had expected. The drink had sharpened his thoughts and senses to the point where he was sure his IQ had increased. He had felt no signs of intoxication or physical impairment, and when his heightened senses had relaxed, he had felt rested rather than hungover. Hopefully there was more of this beverage in the house somewhere because he was sure he was going to need it again.

With the guidance he had received from the two guardians since his initiation, he was experiencing more moments of confidence rather than moments of doubt, and he thought maybe he understood why he had been chosen for this destiny. Everything he had learned was a part of the puzzle that his life on this mountain had always been. The missing fragments were coming into focus and every piece was perfect. Too bad the rest of his life wasn't following suit.

He refocused on his task and scrolled through another screen filled with unread messages. A new email popped up in his inbox. It was from David at Gibson Investments. The subject read: Ski Resort.

> Bob,
> Just wanted to thank you for the heads up on Bradford Development. Turns out he never had the deed. Needless to say, that deal is dead, and the grapevine says you are the one who bought the property. I assume that is why you were not on board with developing the land the last time we spoke. I am hoping I can get you to reconsider. We can help you become a very wealthy man. There is enough land up there we can set aside a nice piece for your private home and still have more than enough for the resort. Let's get together for lunch next week. I'll have my secretary call yours. Looking forward to seeing you again.
> David

Well the answer was unequivocally no. But how was he supposed to tell the investment firm he was building an office complex for, that they couldn't develop the land he had bought out from under them. He blew out a heavy sigh. He was going to have to think about this before he responded.

Beauty trotted to his side and licked his cheek before she sat at his feet and wagged her tail. He smiled and patted her head. He knew what she wanted. His wolf was itching to go outside. He closed his laptop and stretched his cramped muscles before he followed her to the front door.

They stepped across the threshold and Robert felt a strong urge to head toward the lake. He looked at the dock and saw Jeremy pacing at the edge. His heart filled with nervous anticipation. It was time. He exhaled. He hadn't missed his cue.

Beauty kept pace with him the whole way down as she pranced at his side. His canine was in a particularly happy mood today, and she had been since she had roused him just before dawn with a cold, wet nose to the center of his forehead. When he had opened his eyes, she had licked the bridge of his nose.

Despite his wet face he had smiled at her. Her mood had infected him the instant he was awake and he had felt eager to start the day. She had greeted him every morning with a sloppy kiss and it had become something he now looked forward to. His wolf had found a comfortable spot in his world and her happiness had invaded his heart. There was nothing she had done, no matter how annoying it had been, that had failed to bring joy to his soul.

She had been constantly at his side since the night she had shown up at the house, and he had come to expect her unwavering support. She was his defender and protector, and she had stolen his heart completely. The only problem with that was, he was pretty sure she knew it.

He looked down the hill to where Jeremy had stopped pacing at the end of the dock. He was as still as a statue. It was an eerily noticeable characteristic of the souls from the other side. They were uncannily immobile which made it easy to tell the difference between spirits and humans. The forces of nature that caused mortals to constantly move to retain their balance had no effect on spirits, so unless they deliberately moved, their image remained perfectly still.

He and Beauty were halfway to the dock when he felt his confidence waiver. This was his first real test as the Master of DeLancey Manor. He had been executing his duties as the landowner with ease, and of course it was no problem. It was a normal part of life. But now it was time to use the skills Eleanor and Shamus had taught him. It was vital that he got it right and helped Jeremy get through Purgatory.

He took a deep breath and continued toward the dock. He had hoped Nathaniel could have told him exactly what to do. After all, George had said that Nathaniel would take care of this sort of thing. But Nathaniel had explained to him that it was forbidden for a spirit to interfere with a soul's journey to paradise, and that included telling the master of the manor what needed to be done. Nathaniel could neither help nor hinder their progress. However, a mortal could, and that is why it was the master's responsibility to help a soul when it got stalled in Purgatory. He sighed and wondered what else George may have gotten wrong.

He took a moment to banish the other souls from his sight and mind, and smiled when the only one left was Mr. Jeremy Greene. He stepped onto the dock and listened to the cadence of Beauty's nails on the wood until they stopped next to the soul who stood at the end.

"Good morning, Jeremy," Robert said.

"Oh." Jeremy blinked then looked at him. "Hello, Master Robert. I didn't realize I wasn't alone."

Robert smiled. "You must have been deep in thought if you didn't hear Beauty trotting down the dock."

"Well, yes, I have been thinking about what Fr. Kelly said. But the truth is, I didn't hear you coming. My connection to the mortal world is limited and I don't always know what is happening around me."

"What do you mean?"

"I can't hear or see most things like I could when I was alive." He looked out at the lake. "If I concentrate, I can see the water and the trees, but you and Fr. Kelly are the only living souls I can see."

"Living souls?"

"Yes. The other souls I can see are immortal."

"So you *can* see them. I had wondered about that." He paused. "Why don't you speak to them?"

"I don't bother to try anymore since they have never answered me anyway. I guess they can't see me. But it's probably for the best because they don't stay very long." He paused. "Nathaniel said the ones I can see are on their way to Heaven." He turned to face Robert. "I hope I will be able to follow them soon."

"You will." Robert glanced at the dead trunks in the middle of the lake. Repose was invisible. "Can you see Heaven?"

"No." He smiled. "But they showed it to me at my judgement. I was told it is my destiny when I am done here." He looked across the water. "I haven't been there yet, but I miss it." He looked back at Robert. "Isn't that strange?"

"Well, I don't know. I think it sounds more like an excellent tool to keep you motivated." Robert crossed his arms. "So let's get you there before you start to feel like you never will."

"Okay." Jeremy's smile widened.

"Nathaniel told me about your situation and I think I can help."

"That would be great. Fr. Kelly told me it's been eight months since I crossed over."

"Hmm. I find it interesting he would mention that. I thought time didn't matter after death."

"It doesn't really. There's no way to keep track of it, and honestly, I can't tell you exactly when I got here." He frowned. "But hearing that I've been here for eight months sounds like a long time when there's nothing to do but think."

"I suppose it would." Robert paused. "Can you tell me what is keeping you here?"

Jeremy stuffed his hands into his pockets. "I'm not exactly sure. I mean, at the end of my trial the angels told me I had been unfaithful and that I had to lament my sin. But I had already done that. I had regretted being unfaithful to Alice, and that's why I told Genevieve it was over."

"Was your remorse genuine?"

"Yes." Jeremy slumped his shoulders. "The morning before I died, I read Alice's diary. We'd had another fight and I was looking for something to use against her in the divorce. But what I found in there shocked me. I had no idea how much Alice still loved me, and I knew right then I had to go back to her."

"Why were you surprised to find out she still loved you?"

"I thought Alice was the one who wanted out and I was the one dragging my feet." He sat on the end of the dock. "For years it felt like she was trying to push me out of her life. But I couldn't bring myself to let go of her, even though I thought she had stopped loving me."

Robert sat next to Jeremy, and Beauty laid between them with her head on her paws. She closed her eyes and rolled against Robert when he stroked her back.

"Is that why you got involved with Genevieve?" Robert said.

"I guess. I never intended for it to happen, but she was just so amazing to me." He smiled. "Genevieve made me the center of her life and it felt good. And I hadn't had that in a very long time." He paused. "But when I realized there was a chance, a real chance, to save my marriage, I knew I had to try."

"You had decided to repair your marriage and repented for breaking your vows before God."

"Yes."

"Then there must be another sin you are expected to lament." He scratched his chin. "What else happened at your judgement?"

"A lot of great things." Jeremy's eyes glistened. "It was nothing like what I thought it would be. I was shown all the good things I had done in my life and it was so amazing."

"Really?" Robert smiled. "I don't mean to sound surprised. But what made it so amazing?"

"I saw so many things I had done right. Things that I thought were insignificant." His image brightened. "I got to see all the people I had helped when I was working in sales. The funny thing is I thought I was just doing my job, and when I saw their faces, I could hardly believe all that joy was because I had sold a piece of equipment to their doctors." He straightened his shoulders. "And then there were the doctors. I never knew how much they really cared about their patients, especially the ones who had such little hope. But I had delivered the answer to their prayers and helped bring peace to their hearts."

"Wow. That would be an amazing thing to see."

"It was incredible. I was told I had used the charisma God had given me to persuade the medical centers to buy the equipment. And you know, it never occurred to me that I was doing God's work."

"That's nice to hear. It gives me hope for my judgement day." Robert paused. "I suppose if you think about it, we're all more important to this world than we realize."

"Yes…we are." Jeremy's smile started to fade.

"A lot of people were blessed by you and didn't even know it. In fact, I would guess they still don't know it."

"They don't. That's why my deeds are so favorable to God. I was not rewarded for them in life. I will receive my rewards when I get to Heaven."

"Then we better figure out how to get you there." Robert crossed his arms. "There must be something you haven't considered."

"Well, I was told I was unfaithful." He shrugged his shoulders. "I only had one wife. Who else could I have been unfaithful to?"

"Anyone, Jeremy. In the simplest definition, a person can be unfaithful by simply breaking a promise."

"I hadn't thought about it that way."

"Is there an important promise you failed to keep?"

Beauty jumped to her feet and looked toward the line of trees at the end of the drive. A second later Robert heard the engine getting closer. He knew that sound. It was Gracelyn's SUV.

"I don't know," Jeremy said. "Maybe."

"Well, give it some thought." Robert got to his feet. "I'll be back."

"Master Robert." Jeremy stood and faced him. "Could I have just a bit more of your time? It helps me think when I have someone to talk to."

The look on Jeremy's face was sobering. Robert could see the loneliness in his eyes. He had to help him get to Heaven soon.

"I won't be long, Jeremy." He put his hand on his shoulder. "Someone just arrived at the house and I have to speak to them. While I'm gone, think about the ones who were closest to you. That should help."

Robert turned to leave and saw Beauty trotting up the yard. He quickened his pace to catch up with her. He wasn't sure what she was going to do. After all, she wasn't happy with Gracelyn the last time she had come to Cedar Rock. The last thing he wanted to deal with was a dog bite.

4

Forgiveness

Robert hurried up the hill toward the house. Gracelyn had already gotten out of her SUV and had made it up the front steps. When he reached the edge of the driveway, he saw her standing at the threshold with her hand on the door knob. Apparently, she still felt entitled to be in his home without an invitation. That misconception would be corrected today. If she had let herself in, and found the diary on the mantle, he was sure she would have picked it up. Then she would have demanded to know why her mother's entries had been replaced by a long list of names. He couldn't tell her the truth and he wasn't going to start lying to her now. He scowled. Damn her! It was none of her business, anyway. In fact, nothing on this mountain was her business.

Beauty had stopped Gracelyn from getting into the house, and was keeping pace with her as she backed away from the front door. His wolf uttered a soft growl and Gracelyn continued her retreat until she backed into the railing post. The basket she was holding pressed into her belly when she stopped suddenly, and he heard the clink of glass.

"Beauty," Gracelyn said softly, "you know me, girl. I won't hurt you."

She took a cautious step forward and froze when Beauty bared her teeth. She backed up to the post again and kept her eyes on the wolf.

"Bob!" she said. "Are you here?"

He came to a stop at the bottom of the porch stairs and crossed his arms.

"That's as close as you're going to get," he said. "She doesn't let trespassers into the house."

Gracelyn gasped and turned toward him. A champagne flute tipped against the edge of the basket and she caught the crystal before it fell to the ground.

"Oh, Bob, you almost gave me a heart attack."

"I doubt that." He ascended the stairs and stood next to Beauty. "What are you doing here, Gracelyn?"

"I wanted to give you this." She stepped forward and handed him the basket full of goodies. "With all the chaos going on it slipped my mind."

Robert looked at the gift. A bottle of champagne, two flutes with the Great Pines Real Estate logo engraved on them, a small block of cheese, and a packet of over-priced crackers all laid in a bed of green and burgundy confetti.

"Thank you," he said.

"You're welcome." She fidgeted with her keys. "We give a basket to all our clients."

"I'm sure you do, but the fact that you stopped trying to evict me from my home was good enough for me."

She cleared her throat. "Yes, well I uh, wanted you to have it anyway." She pointed to the basket. "There's a card behind the champagne."

Robert set the basket on the glider and opened the blue envelope. The front of the card had a beautiful golden sunset over a snow-covered mountain, and the words 'Even the Hardest Day Can Have a Beautiful Ending' were embossed across the bottom. On the inside she had written, 'Please forgive me. All my love, Gracie'.

He sighed and dropped the card into the basket. When he looked up Nathaniel was standing beside her. She was unnaturally still and the air around him felt stale. He looked out at the lake and the waves had halted their journey toward the shore.

"What's going on?" Robert said.

"I ceased the progression of your world," Nathaniel said. "I am waiting for the soul in Repose."

"I hope this one has an easier task." Robert combed his fingers through his hair and exhaled. "I am still trying to figure out what to say to Jeremy without giving him the answer because I'm pretty sure I know what it is."

"I will admit you have a difficult task."

"Thank you." He paused. "I am surprised there hasn't been another soul needing me before now."

"Souls like Jeremy are the exception. As you have seen, most souls find their way through Purgatory on their own, and usually rather quickly."

Nathaniel greeted Beauty with a scratch behind her ear. She licked the back of his hand and Robert did a doubletake. She had not been frozen with the rest of his world. But then again, he should have expected her to be immune to something like this. She had a connection to the spirit world. He just hadn't figured out what it was yet.

"So what do I need to know about this soul?" Robert said.

"Nothing." Nathaniel jumped onto the railing and sat on his heels to rest his elbows on his knees. "Mrs. Ruth Devonshire has served the Lord well. I will simply escort her to the portal and away she'll go, straight to paradise."

"I don't understand. If you don't need me, why did you stop everything to tell me about her?"

"I did not stop your world to talk about Mrs. Devonshire. I did it so you could keep me company."

"Keep you company?"

"Yes. I find it devilishly boring to wait alone. So, I thought we could chat a while."

"Chat? You're kidding, right?"

"No." Nathaniel grinned. "I am not."

Robert held his tongue and shook his head. "Okay. What do you want to talk about?"

Nathaniel shrugged. "We could talk about the weather, but that would be a bit mundane. Why don't you pick a topic?"

Robert clenched his jaw then rubbed his chin to ease the tension. "I don't mean to be rude, Nathaniel, but I don't think this is a good time for a social call. I was trying to help Jeremy when Gracelyn showed up. So, I came up here to get rid of her only to find out she wants to have a deep conversation about 'us'. Since I can't tell her there is a dead man waiting to talk to me down by the lake, I have to think of something else to tell her so she will go away."

"Well then, we have something to talk about." He jumped down and walked to her. "I am a bit of an expert when it comes to women."

"You?"

"Of course." He walked a full circle around her. "I have been observing them since our Father created Eve."

"I didn't think any amount of time would be enough to figure them out." Robert scowled.

"They are less complicated than mortal men realize. In fact, once you understand their thought process, getting what you want from them becomes the simplest task in the world."

"Really?"

"Yes, really. Now, think about what you want from her?"

"I want her off this mountain."

"She is a woman." Nathaniel grinned. "You will have to be more specific than that."

"You said getting her off this mountain would be simple."

"No. I said getting what you wanted from a woman was simple. I did not say they were simple creatures."

"I want her to go home so I can help Jeremy get through Purgatory."

"Okay." Nathaniel sighed and shook his head. "Let me break this down for you. If you say, 'This is a really bad time for me, love. How about we meet later for dinner?' she'll leave and come back this evening expecting a romantic rendezvous." He leaned his elbow on her shoulder and cocked an eyebrow. "On the other hand, if you tell her to go away because you find her completely repulsive, you probably won't see her ever again."

"I think something in between those two would be what I want."

"Obviously." Nathaniel paced to the top of the stairs and crossed his arms. "Now, beyond wanting her to go home, what else do you want from her?"

Robert looked at her blue eyes. There was sadness in how she gazed at him. They each had so much to regret, and making things right between them seemed impossible.

"What I want from her," he said, "is something she is not willing to give me."

"Her trust," Nathaniel said.

"Yes." Robert stepped closer to her. "She needed the reassurance of a thief before she would believe in me."

"That was a poor decision she made. I will agree with that."

"She believed her brother, Richard, a despicable human being, over me."

"She did. But the situation was overwhelming for her."

"Don't you mean complicated?" Robert smirked.

"Yes. It was complicated for her."

"It should have been simple."

"Why? Because it was for you?"

Robert tried again to put himself in her shoes to understand how she had come to her decision, but he couldn't get past his anger over her betrayal. The pain was too deep.

"You know the reason she is afraid to trust you," Nathaniel continued, "yet you expect her to overlook it." He stepped to Beauty's side. "Like it never happened."

"That's not true. I knew I had to prove myself to her again, and I tried everything to regain her trust." He exhaled. "She just refused to give it to me."

"That is not entirely true either. She did give you her trust again, but she faltered." He paused. "Don't you think she deserves the second chance you want to give her?"

Robert looked at Nathaniel. "You're reading my thoughts."

"I am not, nor will I ever do such a thing." His expression sobered. "Reading a soul's mind without explicit permission is a sin taken very seriously by the Lord. That is a transgression I shall never commit."

"Then how do you always seem to know what is in my head?"

"I know you. I have carried out my task since nearly the dawn of time, and this mountain has always been my home. There is nothing that has happened on this hallowed ground that I have not witnessed." He paused. "You spent most of your childhood here with Gracelyn, you fell in love with her in the forest...and you abandoned her in this manor."

"I did not abandon her." He paused. "She was surrounded by her family."

"Lying is a sin, Master Robert. Even when the only one who could possibly believe such rubbish is you."

"I am not lying. I was barely a man when I left this mountain. I thought I was doing what was best for the both of us." Robert swallowed hard. "I had no idea how much she needed me."

"Ignorance of the consequences of one's sin does nothing to lessen the pain it inflicts on others."

Robert's chest constricted and he looked at her eyes again. Her sadness had started with his selfish act of cowardice.

"So you're saying it is my fault she does not trust me."

"No. Gracelyn is in complete control of her free will. It is for her to decide to trust or not to trust." Nathaniel stood at Robert's side and looked at her. "It is expected by God that each of us forgive the transgressions committed against us. I simply pointed out that you are not without sin against Gracelyn."

Robert hesitated. "Then I must forgive her."

"Yes. For your sake as much as hers."

"I can do that." He paused. "But we have both changed so much. I am not sure I can give her what she wants."

"Then send her away and leave the door half open."

Beauty shoved her nose into Nathaniel's gut and belted out a sassy howl.

"The Lord's will be done, My Lady," he said to her. "The decision is not mine to make."

"Easy, girl." Robert patted her head. "Gracelyn could never take your place in my heart."

"I must go."

A rush of wind slammed into Robert's side and Nathaniel rose off the ground. His wings spanned nearly the width of the house as he swooped down the hill and landed elegantly next to an elderly woman standing on the shore. He bowed to her and kissed the back of her hand, then offered her his arm before he led her toward the trees. As they walked along a sunlit path, she became younger, and when they finally disappeared into the forest, she was a beautiful woman any man could lose his heart to.

Robert smiled. Nathaniel was leading her to the portal. She was entering paradise, and the angel escorting her showered her with love and tenderness, and the respect due a soul God had chosen to enter his kingdom.

A gentle breeze pressed his shirt against his chest and he looked at the water. The waves were flowing to the shore once more. He turned his gaze to Gracelyn and watched her fidget with her keys. He sighed.

"I know what you want, Gracelyn," he said. "But I need some time to think about what I want."

"I understand." She hesitated. "At least we didn't fight this time. Maybe we're making progress."

"Maybe."

They stood in silence for a minute while she looked in every direction but his. When Beauty moved and stood between them, Gracelyn took a step back.

"I don't mean to be rude," he said, "but I am in the middle of something I really need to get back to."

"Oh, of course. I have to get back to the office, too."

She walked to the bottom of the steps and turned toward him.

"Stop in the next time you're in town."

"I will," he said.

Robert waited while she climbed into her SUV, and Beauty took several steps toward the lake. When the vehicle turned the corner at the treeline, his wolf took off for the dock.

He smiled and followed her down the hill. He knew exactly how he was going to help Jeremy. God's plan was indeed perfect because Gracelyn's visit had come at the right time. His conversation with Nathaniel had given him a new point of view in his own life, and that was the key. Even when we are sinned against, we are not without sin ourselves.

How naïve we mortals are, he thought. So quick to find fault in others while so slow to accept responsibility for our own part in the consequences of life. Robert was so far from perfect that he wondered why he had been chosen as the master of the manor. But it was all part of God's plan, wasn't it? Of course, it was, and that was something to hold on to. Robert may not be perfect, but the plan he was a part of, was. And for now, that was all he needed to know.

5

A Cursed Deed

Richard Bradford rubbed his chin and tried his best to feign concern for his father's words. The old man was warning him, again, about the dangers of trespassing on Robert's land. Robert's land, huh? It annoyed him how easily those words rolled off his father's tongue. DeLancey Manor had been in Eleanor Bradford's family for five generations. It was the home she had been raised in, the same home she had raised her own children in. Now, practically overnight, it belonged to Robert Castle, and her widowed husband wasn't the least bit upset about it.

Well the loss of the family estate may not bother his father, but it pissed him the hell off, especially since he had tried so hard for the past sixteen years to get his hands on it. That property should have been given to him. The estate had been handed down to a member of the family in each generation, and he was George and Eleanor's first born. By family tradition alone, the deed should have been signed over to him. Instead, his father had sold his birthright to a man who hid behind his honor like a coward.

As usual, Richard would have to do things the hard way. No problem. That was his specialty. Getting his hands on something this valuable was never easy. But that was what he loved about this game, the challenge of finding the angle no one else had. This time it was as simple as a back door. It turned out there was more than one way up that mountain.

He drummed his fingers on the large envelope on his desk. It held a deed. The deed to a homestead that had been deserted long ago, so long ago in fact, that most people didn't even know it existed. The property was just over the ridge from DeLancey Manor. Robert Castle was no longer the sole resident of Cedar Rock Mountain.

"If this is another one of your underhanded schemes, it's going to blow up in your face," George said. "DeLancey Manor will never belong to you."

"Who said anything about DeLancey Manor?" He crossed his arms.

George shook his head. "You're a fool if you expect me to believe this has nothing to do with getting your hands on the estate."

"Give it a rest, Dad. I got it. The estate is gone." Richard paused. "I still think you made a mistake, but there is nothing I can do about it now." He paced to his office window and gazed out at the busy streets of Capital City. "DeLancey Manor belongs to Robert now. I have accepted that."

"Then stop trying to get on that mountain."

"I'm not trying to get anywhere." He watched a pickpocket work the crowd waiting for a bus, and grinned. He took a good, long look at his face. The young man may prove useful one day. "Fate, or as you like to say, God, gave me the deed for a piece of property up there. Who am I to throw away a gift from God?"

"Yes, well, something isn't right about that. I still don't believe you bought the deed at an estate auction?"

"According to the law, I did." Richard turned around to face his father. "But in all honesty, I had no idea the deed was in that old rolltop desk. The estate furniture was sold as is, which, technically, made everything in it a part of the sale." He grinned. "Including the deed hidden behind the back panel."

"You're losing your touch, son. This lie sounds too much like a fairytale."

"What makes you think I'm lying?"

"Well for one thing, it's what you do best." George crossed his arms. "For another, the claim you filed with the state said you bought it at the Bailey farm auction."

"And?"

"Francis Bailey was dirt poor when he died. The IRS had already taken nearly half of his land for unpaid taxes. No one is going to believe you found a property deed worth a half million dollars in his old rolltop desk."

"Well my guess is he didn't know it was there." He plastered a poorly feigned frown on his face. "But, there's no sense in feeling sorry for him now. He's at peace, right?"

"Yes. I believe he is." George scowled back at him. "But his daughter isn't. If you really did find the deed in Bailey's old desk then that property belonged to him, and his daughter is now the rightful owner."

"Was, dad. She was the rightful owner. But now it seems she has learned a valuable lesson." He winked at his father. "Make sure you clean out a desk before you sell it."

"Have some compassion, Richard. Your soul could benefit from it. That poor girl has a lot of debt to settle for her father's estate. The least you could do is give her a fair price for it."

"Sorry, Dad. The law states the deed belongs to me. She can find some other way to pay off her old man's debts."

"Think of it as charity, then. You don't need that property or the money from selling it off." He paused. "Use it as a tax write-off. Give it to her to sell."

"That's a pretty generous gift for a woman I don't even know."

"You don't have to know someone to help them out."

"There are plenty of organizations that make it their business to help the poor. Bradford Development Group makes a substantial donation to many of them every year, and that is sufficient for my tax purposes. I am not responsible for rescuing every poor person who passes my way."

"You're right. You're not." He paused. "But maybe this gift from God was not meant for you to keep. Maybe you are an answer to her prayers."

"Spare me the sermon."

"It's not a sermon, Richard. I truly believe this is a chance for you to redeem yourself in the eyes of Heaven." He frowned. "Save your soul. Give the deed back to her."

"No. I'll worry about the next life when it comes. For now, I'm focused on the life I'm living, and I didn't get where I am today by giving away assets to people who obviously can't manage their own money."

"Francis Bailey did not mismanage his money. Life threw him an obstacle he couldn't overcome." George shook his head. "Life is not fair, son. A lot of people end up in bad situations through no fault of their own. He did everything he could and it just wasn't enough."

"I fail to see how any of this obligates me to surrender a very valuable piece of land to an estate with more debts than assets."

"For once in your life, Richard, listen to me." George smiled. "You have a wonderful opportunity here. You are in a position to help a young woman through a very difficult time in her life. Son, you can do for her something her father could not."

"And what's in it for me?"

George rolled his eyes. "First and foremost, it just might keep your lousy butt out of hell."

"Don't worry, old man. I've got that covered."

"You can't get into heaven on your own terms, Richard. It doesn't work that way."

"Watch me."

George stepped close to him and gazed into his eyes. A deep sadness emanated from his stare.

"What happened to you, Richard?" George paused. "When did you lose your soul?"

"I haven't lost anything, Dad. I just refuse to be a stooge."

"Being generous with your good fortune makes you a good man, not a stooge."

Richard picked up his copy of the legal papers his attorney had filed with the state and held them up to his father's line of vision.

"This property is worth millions, and until yesterday, it was controlled by the state's wildlife preservation agency." He tossed them back onto his desk. "If I give the deed back to the Bailey estate, the government will give them the measly six figures they tried to give me. I can sell it for ten times what they say it is worth."

"Then give it to Mr. Bailey's daughter and let her sell it."

"You're not getting it, Dad. Giving this land to Bailey's daughter would not make me a generous man, it would make me a fool."

"Better to be a fool in heaven than a wise man in hell."

"Drop it, Dad. It never legally belonged to her anyway."

"Of course, it did, son. It was in her father's desk. It was a part of his estate."

"Not according to the title search." Richard sat back in his leather chair and propped his heels on the end of his desk. "I had the deed researched. The last registered owner died in 1898. She was a widow with no heirs, and she had no ties to the Baileys. I assume she is the one who hid the deed in the desk, and most likely died before anyone knew it was there. Since then, it has been passed around from one auction to the next." He smiled. "I just happen to be the one to find it."

Richard watched his father shake his head and pace to the other end of his office. He knew his story wasn't sitting well with the old man, but it was the best he could do when his father had shown up unannounced. For decades Richard had been lying to his family about one matter or another, especially when he needed them to keep their noses out of his business. In the past, his lies were always planned ahead and well-rehearsed, but this time his father had caught him off guard and he'd had to improvise instead.

"By the way," Richard said, "how did you find out I had this deed?"

"Gracie told me." George turned around and faced his son. "Since she was the agent representing the buyer of DeLancey Manor, she received a copy of the letter the state sent to Robert."

Richard stood and leaned forward on his desk. "Why the hell would they send a letter to him?"

"Because he is the property owner of DeLancey Manor." George smiled and paced to the other side of the desk. "There is a little county ordinance up there you must have overlooked when you were making big plans for your ski resort."

"And what ordinance is that?"

"When a property is sold or changes hands, all the neighbors with shared property lines are notified." George ticked off the points on the fingers of his right hand. "They are given the names of the seller and the buyer, the location of the property, and the current assessment value."

"What moron came up with that ridiculous ordinance?"

"Beats me." George shrugged his shoulders. "It's always been that way."

Richard dropped back into his chair and pushed out a heavy sigh, then glared at his father.

"Are there any other ancient rules and regulations I should know about?"

"Probably," George said. "With the exception of DeLancey Manor, that whole mountain is designated as a natural preserve, which means, that piece of land you refuse to let go of has been managed by the state for a very long time. You might want to do a little more research before you take your bulldozers up there." He winked. "Your little pot of gold might just turn out to be nothing more than a pile of dirt on a very big hill."

"You would love that, wouldn't you?"

"Only if it gave you a change of heart. Because despite everything you've done..." George's smile dissolved. "Even the terrible things I never thought a child of mine could do, I still love you, son."

Richard looked away and clenched his jaw. This father and son talk had served its purpose. For now, his father believed he had found the deed in Mr. Bailey's old desk. Mission accomplished.

"I pray for you every day, Richard," George said.

"That's wonderful, Dad. I'm glad you found a purpose in life."

Richard threw him a sarcastic smile and reached into his pocket when he heard his phone ring.

"Don't give up on yourself, son," George said. "It's never too late to ask for His forgiveness."

The caller ID brought a smile to Richard's face. He looked up at his father and nodded his head toward the door.

"I'll try to remember that, old man. But right now, I have to take care of some business." He connected the call. "This is Bradford."

"Did you secure the deed?"

Richard stood silent and waited for his father to leave. George hesitated at the threshold then dropped his head and closed the door behind him.

"I said, did you secure the deed?"

"Yes. My attorney called me this morning. The state has agreed to release the property."

"Excellent. You know what to do next."

"I'm on my way."

"Make sure you are not followed."

"Relax. I got this. There isn't a set big enough in this city to cross me."

Richard disconnected the call and locked the papers in the safe behind him. The sun had risen above the rooftops and its golden rays had started their journey up Main Street. By noon Capital City would be flooded with light and he would be crossing the Titan River. He hated long road trips, particularly when he had to drive. But this sixteen-hour journey would be worth it. He would be there before sunrise and have a couple hours to sleep. Then the search would begin, and the destiny he had been chasing his whole life would finally be his.

6

The Rock

Derrick sat in the last pew in St. James Church and wrote as fast as he could. The scene had come to him when he was studying the new stained-glass window near the front of the church, and the details were flooding his mind. Inspiration for his new novel had been coming from unexpected places, and he had learned to carry a small notebook with him. In fact, he had scrapped his original idea just last week and had let this new inspiration take on a life of its own. He was curious to see where it would go.

The window in St. James was the latest in more than a dozen religious objects that had given birth to amazing ideas. This time it was the introduction of a new character. He scribbled the last sentence and exhaled as he looked up at the colorful piece of art. Maybe he should thank the mayor for inspiring his new hero. Six months ago, the century's old window had been shattered into a million pieces when the mayor had sent his homerun ball sailing over the fence in the baseball field just behind the church. The star-studded event of local doctors, attorneys, and the like, was a fundraiser for repairs to the church. Despite the forgiveness offered by the pastor, the mayor's guilt had led to the purchase of the new, stunningly beautiful depiction of The Holy Trinity.

A door creaked and soft footsteps approached him from behind. It was Fr. Kelly. He always wore leather slippers in the chapel. The pastor didn't like the echo of footsteps on the hard granite floors through the open space. God's house was meant for silent meditation, not a grand entrance, he once explained. Although in Derrick's opinion, St. James wasn't actually large enough to make any kind of grand entrance, since it only took the priest about twenty steps to reach him. Fr. Kelly genuflected and sat next to him in the pew.

"Is that your latest work?" the pastor said.

"Yes." Derrick handed the notebook to him. "You might actually like this one."

Fr. Kelly skimmed through the pages and smiled. "I think you're right. I look forward to reading it when it's done."

"Well, I'll have to see what my publisher thinks about it." He took the book back from the pastor. "This one is writing itself, and it's nothing like the others I've written for them."

"They will like this one."

"I appreciate the vote of confidence." Derrick said.

"That is not my opinion." He sat back and crossed his arms. "I heard that from a higher authority."

"Really?" Derrick smiled. "Is that why you asked me to meet you here? God told you my book would be a success?"

"No." He smiled back. "And I did not hear it from God. I got that tidbit through the regular channel."

"A channel, huh? You mean like a messenger?" Derrick cocked his head and looked at the stained-glass window again. "Maybe that's my problem. I've been waiting for Him to talk to me himself."

"He has been talking to you, Derrick. You just haven't been listening."

"Is that right?" Derrick smirked. "He should try speaking a little louder because I haven't heard a thing."

Fr. Kelly shook his head. "You know, it is conversations like this one that make me wonder if you ever paid attention in my catechism classes." He paused. "God's voice is not audible. He speaks to your heart and your mind."

"I paid attention." Derrick dropped his gaze to the floor. "I've just never been able to do that."

"I know." He paused again. "That's why I asked you to come here."

"You found a 'Listening to God for Dummies' book?"

Fr. Kelly laughed. "No. I'm here to give you a message, and since you are not listening to Him, He asked me to give it a try."

"God has a message for me, huh?" He looked at the window of the Holy Trinity. "I hope it's more than just a sales projection for my new book."

"That would be unnecessary," he said. "You have used the talent He gave you very well. Your labor will bear the same fruit as before."

"Well, I have you and mom to thank for that. Between her premonitions, and your encouragement, I never would have gotten my first book published." He sat back and smiled. "You know, there were days I thought you were just as clairvoyant as my mother was."

"Why is that?"

"You always seemed to know exactly what I needed to hear."

"Those were not my words. God told me what you needed to hear."

"Really? You must be pretty good at this listening to God thing."

"Well, it is kind of a job requirement."

"I didn't know priests were required to speak with God." Derrick grinned. "So, do you all have staff meetings with the Big Guy, or is it more like a one-on-one?"

Fr. Kelly laughed again. "The only staff meeting I attend is with the Bishop. God speaks to me privately."

"That must be nice."

"It is."

"So, Is this like a daily thing?"

"He speaks to me when He needs me to do something."

"And He wants you to talk to me?"

"Yes. He wants you to do something for Him."

"Really?" Derrick laughed. "Okay, lay it on me. What does The Big Guy want me to do?"

"I'm serious, Derrick. The Lord has a job for you."

"I already have one. You know that." Derrick hesitated. "Writing is what I am meant to do, and pardon me for saying so, but I am damn good at it."

"We all know what a wonderful writer you are." Fr. Kelly crossed his arms. "God does not want you to stop writing. He wants you to do both."

"Both? Don't you think that's asking a bit much? Writing takes a lot of my time, especially this latest one."

"Yes, I know. This new book has taken a tremendous amount of your time, hasn't it?"

"Yes, it has, but sometimes writing is like that. Inspiration is like a feast and famine kind of thing. It doesn't follow regular schedules."

"Neither does The Lord. But His timing is always perfect." Fr. Kelly looked sideways at him. "Wouldn't you agree?"

"That's what you always said. But I can't speak from experience."

"Do you honestly believe that?"

"Well, I don't know." He shifted uncomfortably. "I guess I just haven't needed Him to do anything for me yet."

"Good heavens, Derrick. Open your eyes." He turned to face him. "Do you honestly think it was a coincidence that Dean Witherby decided to go to confession at St. Patrick's Cathedral when you just happened to be the only other soul in that church?"

"What?" Derrick recalled his impersonation of a priest in the confessional and looked away. "How did you know about that?"

"He showed me what happened in a vision."

"A vision?" Derrick stood and began pacing in the aisle. "You saw me—I didn't plan that, you know. He backed me into a corner and I..."

"You did what The Lord needed you to do." Fr. Kelly smiled. "Although, I wouldn't make a habit of impersonating a priest, if I were you. You weren't very convincing."

Derrick stopped pacing and smiled.

"Mr. Witherby was convinced," he said.

"There was a lot of divine intervention helping with that."

"Aw, come on, I was pretty good. I just repeated a lot of what you always say."

"Just promise you won't repeat that sin."

"Sin?" Derrick started to pace again. "But you said I did what He needed me to do. Doesn't that mean God wanted me to do that?"

"He needed you to hear the truth. He didn't intend for you to absolve sin without the authority to do so."

"Shit," he whispered.

"Don't be upset, Derrick. Your sin has been forgiven."

"But what about Witherby? He thinks a real priest absolved his sin." Derrick combed his fingers through his hair. "Geezus. I didn't mean for this to happen."

"Relax. Dean Witherby has been forgiven."

"How? You said yourself I didn't have the authority to do" – he waived his hands in circles – "that."

"I told you. There was a lot of divine intervention helping you that day."

He blew out a heavy breath. "I hope so."

The two sat in silence and Derrick thought about how God had orchestrated his life that day. He hadn't planned to go to Capital City, let alone to St. Patrick's Cathedral. But then he found himself in the old Romanesque style chapel that day getting inspiration for what would become his current work in progress. While he was there, the drafter who had helped his brother try to frame Robert, had shown up to confess his sins. God had given Derrick the truth on a silver platter, along with the start of his new book.

"I never thought God played such a subtle role in my life."

"I suppose you were waiting for Him to descend from the clouds in all His Glory and speak to you as I am doing right now."

"Well, yeah." Derrick felt the sting of humiliation in his gut. "It sounds kinda stupid when you say it out loud, doesn't it?"

"Maybe." Fr. Kelly smiled. "But it's not far from what most people expect. They keep looking for the obvious instead of the subtle."

"Then why doesn't He just talk to us?"

"Because if He did, there would be no point in having free will, would there? We would all just do what He tells us to do." He looked up at the crucifix behind the altar. "If we are given the answers to the test, what is the point of the test? You cannot be a doctor, a lawyer, or an architect without first proving you are worthy of such a station. Therefore, it seems only right that we must all show we are worthy of heaven by passing the test God has laid before us, don't you think?"

"Sometimes that test is too hard for me. I don't think I can pass it without a little help."

"That's why He sent me to you. I am a messenger of God."

"A messenger of God, huh?" Derrick leaned his elbows on his knees. "So what's this job he wants me to do?"

"Well, it's rather complicated, and it requires a lot of concentration. Since you are not the master of the manor, this won't be an easy task for you."

"The master of the manor?"

"Yes." Fr. Kelly kept his gaze fixed on the crucifix. "Have you made things right between you and Robert Castle yet?"

"What? I..." Derrick shook his head. "I thought you were giving me my message."

"Answer my question, Derrick."

The priest had not blinked since he had set his gaze on the image of Jesus. Derrick slid to the front of the pew and looked at his face. The old man wasn't old anymore. He was young. The wrinkles at the corners of his eyes were gone, and the gray flecks in his hair had turned white and were overtaking the sandy brown that had well outnumbered the gray only a moment ago. His eyes had become a brilliant sky blue, and he smiled as he turned to look at Derrick.

"What the…" Derrick stood up and took a step back. "Who – what are you?"

"I am a messenger angel," he said.

"Holy shit," Derrick whispered. "You're a real angel… like from heaven."

"Yes. Although, it is rare that I reveal myself to mortals."

"Mortals?" He raised his eyebrows. "So, you're dead?"

"No. I am certainly not dead. I am an inhabitant of Heaven. There is no death in Heaven."

"I see. So, you're a messenger angel disguised as a priest."

"You could say that."

"Then what makes it okay for you and not me?"

Fr. Kelly laughed. "You never miss a detail."

"I try not to."

"Well then, since you asked. My ordination came from Heaven, not the mortal world."

"Wow. I didn't know they made priests in Heaven." Derrick retraced the conversation to the point he was truly interested in. "So this message you have for me, what is it?"

"What do you know about Purgatory?"

"More questions." Derrick groaned. "I know how to spell it."

"Wonderful. I'll give you an A on your spelling test." The angel rolled his eyes. "Anything else?"

"It's where we go if we aren't sinful enough to be cast into hell, but we're also not good enough for Heaven."

"Oh boy." The angel shook his head and exited the pew. "I knew I should have checked with Eleanor first."

"What did you say?"

"I should have checked with your mother before I met with you."

"My mother?" Derrick moved into the aisle to face him and hesitated before he closed the distance between them. "You can speak to my mother?" he whispered.

"Yes. Of course." He cocked his head. "You doubt that your mother went to Heaven?"

"No, not at all." Derrick could feel his heart thumping against his ribs. "I just didn't know you knew her."

"For Heaven's sake, why wouldn't I know her? We're both inhabitants of Heaven–" He held up his hand to halt Derrick's response. "Never mind. I forgot. Mortal logic gets in your way of understanding such things."

"What the heck is mortal logic?"

"It's nothing. Forget I said that."

"Well, can you tell me?" Derrick hesitated. "Is she... is she happy?"

"She is in Heaven, my dear boy." He smiled. "She is exceedingly happy."

"Good." Derrick swallowed the painful lump in his throat. She must not miss him. "I'm glad to hear that."

"Yes, well I can see you have a rather healthy share of mortal logic so let's go back to the beginning and try this another way."

"You said it again, mortal logic. What is that?"

"That is a discussion for another time." He scratched his chin. "For now, may I assume you made peace with Robert Castle?"

"Wait – what? We were talking about my mother and the message you have for me. What does any of this have to do with Bob Castle?"

"Try to keep up with me."

"I am, but you certainly aren't making it easy."

"May the blessed saints give me strength," the angel whispered. He grew several inches in size to look down at Derrick and forced a smile while he spoke. "Are you still at odds with Robert Castle or are you capable of having a civil conversation with him?"

Derrick took a half step back to keep from having to look up at Fr. Kelly, and thought about the last time he had spoken to Bob. He had run into him at the hardware store in Crescent Valley about a week after the truth had come out. The conversation was brief, and Derrick had actually admitted he was wrong. Then they shook hands and went their separate ways.

"We're good," he said. "There're no hard feelings between us."

"Excellent." The angel returned to his mortal size. "You will be needed on the mountain later this week. A good time to arrive would be Friday afternoon."

"Needed for what?" He raised his eyebrows. "I said we were good. I didn't say we were best friends."

"God knows what He is doing, Derrick. Have faith in His plan." He winked. "And a little less of that mortal logic, huh?"

The angel turned and headed toward the altar.

"Wait, um, sir." Derrick followed him. "What am I supposed to do when I get there?"

"Have faith, Derrick." He smiled. "All it takes is a little faith."

The angel resumed his journey forward and genuflected toward the tabernacle. When he rose, the old man called Fr. Kelly turned toward Derrick.

"Hold tight to that mustard seed." He smiled. "It will keep you focused."

The priest disappeared into the sacristy, and Derrick scratched his temple. Something touched his cheek and pulled his hand back to look at it. An acrylic charm dangled from a sterling silver chain. In the center of the charm was a tiny mustard seed.

"A little faith is all it takes, huh?" he whispered. "I can do that."

He tucked his notebook under his arm and headed for the door. He had a few things to finish up before he started his new job.

7

Revelation

Robert reached the lake and saw Beauty resting next to Jeremy at the end of the dock. His shoulders were slumped just enough Robert could picture him holding a fishing pole and waiting for that first tug on the line. The pair looked content. In front of them a line of ducklings rode the gentle waves as they followed their mother to the boathouse. The morning sun had risen above the evergreens on the eastern edge and a golden shimmer danced across the water. Robert looked up and saw the wind sway through the treetops as it whispered a secret to the heavens, and a chorus of birdsongs echoed the sentiment. The air was a pleasant temperature and when the wind dipped to the ground, it wrapped around him like the arms of a loving parent. He closed his eyes and pulled in a deep breath to receive the splendor of God's creation.

When he opened his eyes again, he exhaled a contented sigh because he felt blessed to have been given this moment. He was surrounded by the majesty of God, the subtle elements that were combined to create this day, and he was so grateful to have been given this chance to soak it all in. But then he noticed the perfect stillness of Jeremy's posture and sighed. The soul sitting next to Beauty could no longer enjoy the simple wonders of this mortal world, and Robert hoped he had taken the time, at least once while he was alive, to take notice. Then Robert vowed to look harder at the quiet details around him as often as he could, so he could experience even the smallest of God's miracles before it was too late.

He stepped onto the wood and heard Jeremy speak.

"I used to think I was pretty smart," he said. "But now I'm beginning to wonder if I'm just too stupid to know I'm stupid."

Beauty uttered three quick moans and Jeremy laughed.

"I guess you're right," Jeremy said. "I can't give up yet. But I've been trying to figure this thing out for so long. If Master Robert can't help me find the answer, I have a feeling I'll be spending my eternity right here."

Beauty jumped to her feet when Robert stopped behind them and greeted him with a press of her muzzle against his abdomen. He stroked her shoulder and smiled at Jeremy when he stood to face him.

"Don't worry, Jeremy," Robert said. "I'm betting you'll be in Heaven before sunset."

"Really?"

Jeremy smiled and his whole body brightened. It was as if doubt had dulled the image of his spirit and now the light of hope was shining inside him.

"Come with me," Robert said. "I want to show you something."

Jeremy walked at his side but was careful to stay at least a half-step behind. Robert struggled to maintain a normal cadence and fought the urge to slow his pace. All this "Master Robert" stuff was going to take some getting used to, and he had serious doubts he would ever be worthy of the respect that was being heaped upon him. After all, they were the supernatural spirits with powers he could only gape at, while he was the mere mortal.

They crossed the threshold of the house and Jeremy came to a halt.

"Wow," he said. "Is this Heaven?"

Robert watched him look over the entire room. It was like watching a man drink his first glass of water after being in the desert for too long.

"No." He grinned. "This is DeLancey Manor."

"It's beautiful." Jeremy looked at Robert. "I can see everything. I even smell... raspberries."

"You can thank Nathaniel for that." Robert placed his hand on Jeremy's shoulder. "Follow me."

They turned left into the dining room. Beauty darted ahead of them and jumped up on the window seat, the exact spot where Robert planned to sit. He shook his head. It might be a sin for a spirit to read another soul's mind, but he was going to have to ask about canines. His wolf seemed to know his thoughts before he did, and if she kept talking to spirits, she just might tell them something he didn't want them to know.

"My youthful perception of life came to an end in this very spot," Robert said. "I was eighteen years old when I made a decision that changed, not only my life, but the life of someone I loved."

Robert settled next to Beauty and waited for Jeremy to sit on the chair across from them.

"It is a story I want to tell you," Robert continued, "because I think it will give you a new perspective. But first you need to know a little bit about me so you can understand why my decision was so important."

Jeremy stayed silent and a look of hope filled his expression.

"I spent a great deal of my childhood on this mountain," Robert said, "even though I lived on a ranch in the valley."

"Ranching is a lot of work," Jeremy said. "When did you get the time to do anything else?"

"I had more free time than I should have. My childhood was pretty easy and somedays I wonder where I got my ambition from."

"What do you mean?"

"I am the youngest of five boys. My brothers are all much older than me, and they were already taking care of the ranch by the time I came along. They didn't have the patience for a little boy with an abundance of curiosity, so my parents sent me off with anyone who was willing to take me for the day."

Jeremy frowned. "That sounds kind of sad. Like you weren't wanted by your own family."

"I suppose it does." Robert shrugged. "But I was more than happy to get out of doing chores, so it just never crossed my mind to find offense in being sent away all the time."

"Where did you go?"

"Up here to DeLancey Manor, mostly. When I was born this house was owned by George and Eleanor Bradford." He paused. "Eleanor took me as often as she could, and some Saturday mornings she even showed up at the ranch just after sunrise to pick me up." He smiled. "She treated me the same as she did her own children, and I even called her mom for a while. To be honest, I think I loved her as much as I did my own mother... maybe even a little more."

"How many children did Eleanor have?"

"Three. The oldest of her two sons was my best friend up until high school. We lost touch after graduation." Robert leaned forward and rested his elbows on his knees. "Her daughter, Gracelyn, is the one I want to tell you about."

"You hurt her," Jeremy said.

Robert hesitated. "It's a very serious sin to read another soul's mind without permission. You do know that, don't you?"

"Yes." Jeremy sat up straight. "The consequences are severe. I won't forget that when I receive the gift."

"Receive the gift? You mean you didn't read my mind?"

"No, Master Robert, I am not able to do that. Even though I lost my mortal senses when I entered Purgatory, I won't be given my heavenly senses until I reach paradise."

"Are you saying you have no senses at all?"

"Well, no." He paused. "The best way I can explain it is, when all the noise went away my mind started noticing other things."

"What do you mean?"

"When I stopped seeing, hearing, and feeling everything around me, the things that were left weren't a mystery anymore."

"I'm not following you," Robert said.

"Without mortal senses there is nothing to distract me. I can focus a hundred percent of my attention on things like her." He pointed to Beauty.

"I suppose that would explain your conversation with her down by the dock. You two were talking to each other."

"Well, she doesn't talk, exactly."

"But she communicated something to you, and you understood her language."

"Yes, but it's not a language like you think. She uses more than just her voice. It's a deeper way to communicate with her whole being, and since all I see and hear is her, every detail in her voice and her body language is clear." He smiled. "She is actually very expressive."

Robert laughed. "She does do a good job of getting her point across."

"Yes, especially her emotions. Her affection for you is undeniable." Jeremy looked at Robert. "Forgive me for saying so, Master Robert, but so is the guilt in your eyes."

Robert hesitated. "So that's how you knew I had hurt Gracelyn. You saw it in my expression."

"Yes, it appeared the moment you said her name. It's the same dark spot I see in my own reflection in the lake." He frowned. "The difference is, I don't know what my guilt is for."

"Well I am hoping my story will help you find the answer. If not, maybe being in this house will help. I always felt DeLancey Manor was a great place to sit and think about things." Robert stood and paced to the front window. "Or maybe it is this mountain. It has always been special to me. As strange as it might sound, I always felt like I was a child of the earth here."

"Nothing sounds strange to me anymore." Jeremy smiled.

"I guess it wouldn't." Robert leaned his back against the windowsill. "Anyway, I felt happiest when I was in the forest. I explored it every chance I got and brought my discoveries back here to study them. Then, one day as I was heading off on another adventure, Gracelyn asked if she could come along. At first, I didn't want to take her because I thought she would find my love of the land weird, but against my better judgement I agreed. Then something wonderful happened. She confessed to me how much she loved Cedar Rock Mountain."

"I know what you mean." Jeremy's smile widened. "I remember the first time I met

Genevieve. It was at a conference in Chicago. While everyone else was having drinks at the bar, I was in a corner booth flipping through catalogs. When she came over to my table I thought she was going to rib me about being a nerd, but instead she sat down and showed me all the things she was excited about."

"It's an amazing feeling when you find a woman who shares your passion," Robert said.

"Yes, it is. I think that's why it all happened, you know? My affair with her. Alice never tried to understand my excitement about my work. She would always walk away when someone asked me what I did for a living." He shrugged his shoulders. "I loved talking about it, but I guess it bored her."

"So you started spending time with Genevieve because she shared your passion."

"Yes. Then one day it happened. I didn't even think about what I was doing until I was lying next to her. She was still asleep when I left her apartment." He looked away. "I didn't want to see her again because I knew it would only make things worse. But I couldn't stop. She just made me feel so good about myself."

"And eventually you fell in love."

"Yes." He looked at Robert. "I denied it for a long time because I would still think about Alice when I was making love to Genevieve. I never stopped loving Alice and I didn't think it was possible to be in love with two women at the same time. So, I kept telling myself Genevieve was just an affair."

"What changed your mind?"

"Alice and I went away for a weekend. I wanted to know if she still loved me. Genevieve was talking about getting married." He looked away. "I had to know for sure my marriage was really over before I committed to her."

"That was when Alice found out about the affair."

"Yes. The weekend was over before it started. We argued about it for hours until she finally won." He closed his eyes. "She told me she had never loved me, and that she wished our daughter wasn't mine."

Robert exhaled. "I'm sorry, Jeremy. I can only imagine how much that must have hurt."

A tiny white spark flashed in the corner of Jeremy's eye when he opened them, and a glittery substance spread in a line down his cheek.

"The four-hour drive home was hell. Neither of us spoke a word to the other." He paused. "I met with my attorney the next morning and moved on with Genevieve like my marriage had never happened."

"But it had happened."

"Not as far as I was concerned. I treated it like a dissolution of a business partnership." The shimmering tear disappeared and Jeremy looked at Robert once again. "I had never told Genevieve I was married, and after what Alice had said to me, I didn't feel there was any need to tell her about it. I moved in with Genevieve a week later and asked her to marry me that night."

"How long did you pretend Alice didn't exist?"

"As long and as often as I could. She didn't know who Genevieve was, and fortunately for me she was a terrible detective. I got a new phone and told Genevieve I had lost the old one. So, Alice contacted me on the old phone and Genevieve never suspected a thing."

"What about your daughter? Did you tell Genevieve about her?"

"No." Jeremy leaned forward and looked down. "Alice told her what I had done and she refused to talk to me. I think she wished I wasn't her father too."

"I know it probably felt that way. But you know it's not true."

Jeremy huffed out a quick laugh. "I do now." He stood and walked to the window next to Robert. "So what happened with you and Gracelyn? Did you..."

"Leave her for another woman? No. I left her because I was afraid." Robert sighed. "We were together for almost four years. She loved me as much as I loved her, maybe even more. But love is never easy, and just like you, it didn't stop me from making the wrong decision."

"You can't compare yourself to me, Master Robert. I had made a commitment to Alice before God, and I broke that commitment."

"I'm not talking about Alice."

"But Alice is the one I was married to. She is the one I vowed to be faithful to until we parted in death."

"And what did you vow to Genevieve?"

"Nothing."

"Really? Because I had made a vow to Gracelyn. We weren't married, but she had given her heart to me." He squared his stance with Jeremy's and looked him in the eye. "I had promised her a thousand times I would always be there for her. That was a vow, and she trusted me to keep it. But when she needed me the most, I ran." He paused. "And not once did I think about the vow I had broken."

Jeremy's complexion dulled. "I didn't want to hurt Genevieve," he whispered.

"But you did."

"You don't understand. We hadn't fully committed to each other. We hadn't said our vows. We weren't married yet."

"In man's eyes, no." Robert took a step back. "But what about in God's eyes?"

Jeremy hesitated. "The angels told me I had a covenant with two women. I didn't understand what that meant."

"Your heart had not renounced your wife, yet you were living with Genevieve. You had made a life with a new love without leaving the old love behind."

"No. Alice told me she didn't love me anymore. I thought it was over."

"But your heart was still with her."

"I couldn't help it. I tried to stop loving her, but I just couldn't."

"And while your heart was still with your wife, you took refuge in the heart of another woman... and together you created another life."

"I didn't know Genevieve was pregnant."

"Would it have made a difference if you had?"

"I don't know." He paused. "When I saw the hour of my death, I saw her holding my hand as she had cried. She had planned to tell me about the baby that night, but I had broken her heart before she'd had the chance to say anything."

"You were in a hurry to go to Alice. Genevieve had tried to interrupt you."

"I wish she had tried harder. If she would have told me first, we could have worked things out, maybe. I don't know what I would have done, but I do know I would never have abandoned my child."

"Maybes and would haves carry no weight in the eyes of heaven," Robert said. "Besides, your sin is against Genevieve, not your unborn child."

"And what about her sin against me? She took my life."

"When the time comes, Genevieve will have her judgement. Until then, she must live with her guilt." Robert sighed. "As for now, you must understand your transgression."

"I do, and I was trying to make things right, for everyone."

"You were trying to make things right for you and Alice, but you didn't consider the other woman who had given you her heart." He sighed. "Think about it, Jeremy. Why did Genevieve poison you?"

"She said I had betrayed her just like I had betrayed my wife."

"And did you?"

Time halted in a silent moment and Robert watched Jeremy's expression change.

"Yes..." Jeremy's eyes filled with shimmering tears. "I led her to her sin, didn't I?"

"What do you think?"

"I think I did." He paused. "Genevieve was such a tender soul. She gave me love when I needed it, and a home when I didn't have one."

"She loved you with every bit of herself."

"Yes, she did, and in return I made her promises I wasn't sure I could keep... some I didn't want to keep."

"Do you understand your sin?"

"Yes," Jeremy whispered. "I took her heart, her love, and her soul. I promised her we would be one and then I destroyed all her dreams when I told her I was going back to Alice." He paused. "I broke my vow to her."

Jeremy took a deep breath - the first Robert had seen him take - and he clenched his chest.

"Oh God! What have I done?"

Robert watched a tear drop from each of Jeremy's eyes and travel slowly down his cheeks. His spirit darkened and he almost disappeared from Robert's sight. Then a brilliant spark of light burst from his chest and his image reappeared in vibrant color. A light shone around him and immense joy radiated so strongly from his being that Robert could feel it.

"Congratulations, Master Robert." Nathaniel stepped to Robert's side. "You have given Heaven a guardian angel."

"Wow." A tingling sensation ran through his limbs. "I did it," he whispered.

"Of course, you did. The Lord does not make mistakes." Nathaniel smiled. "Now I must put him to work. David is about to be born."

"My son!" Jeremy said.

A torrent of light rushed from Jeremy's body and shoved Robert back against the windowsill. The sense of joy that slammed into him was almost too much to bear. His heart hammered against his ribs and his jaw ached with the force of the smile he couldn't contain. It was like nothing he had ever felt before.

"Okay," Nathaniel said, "lesson number one. Don't thrust your emotions at mortals."

Nathaniel laid his hand over Robert's heart and a sense of peace filled his chest. The intense joy was gone and what was left was pure tranquility.

"Thank you," Robert said.

"You are very welcome." Nathaniel bowed to Robert then turned to Jeremy. "We must go now," he said. "David needs you."

Robert watched the two souls dissolve from his sight and Beauty stroked her muzzle against his chest. He slid down the window frame to sit on the sill and held her face in his hands.

"Is that what Heaven feels like?" He stroked her satiny fur. "I'm pretty sure you've been there, so how in the world could you have ever left that place?"

Beauty pushed through his hold and pressed the top of her head against his cheek. He kissed her muzzle and she licked him from his chin to his forehead. He laughed and slid down the wall to sit on the floor. She laid across his lap and he held her tight. The sense of love, acceptance, and security he felt from her was perfect.

"You are my gift from Heaven, Beauty." He buried his face in her fur. "And I will cherish you forever."

8

The Calm

Robert leaned back against the armrest of the couch and watched the flames lick the wood in the fireplace. He smiled and took another sip of the raspberry schnapps Shamus had brought up from the wine cellar. According to the guardian, the spirit had been perfectly aged, and was ready to be replaced. Then he had wasted no time in showing Robert how to make another batch.

Shamus had prefaced his instructions with a tale of how the recipe had been given to his family many centuries ago by a mysterious traveler with supernatural powers. It sounded more like an urban legend, but Robert couldn't help but wonder if there was some truth hidden in the story since the effects of the liquor were nothing like what they should be. Truth or fiction aside, he intended to master the process of distilling because he had no intention of running out of raspberry schnapps.

He set the glass on the end table and inhaled a deep cleansing breath. In addition to heightening his senses, the liquor had a calming effect that had made it easier for him to deal with the problems he'd had at the office. After the blueprints for the ski resort had been proven to be a forgery, there were the issues of theft and disloyalty to deal with at his firm.

In the end, he had demoted one of his drafters, Dean Witherby, after the young man had confessed to stealing the blueprint paper for Richard Bradford. Robert's first instinct had been to fire him and blackball him from the industry. But Dean had reminded Robert of himself when he had first started out. He remembered how hard it was to get ahead in this business, and how tempting it could be to bend the rules to gain an advantage over the competition. He also knew how skilled Richard was at manipulating people, and a part of him felt sorry for Dean for having to deal with a snake like Richard. So instead, he had made a deal with the young drafter. Robert had agreed to keep him on at an intern level and to give him the chance to earn back the trust he had violated. In return, Dean had repeated his confession at a staff meeting to dispel the rumors that were eating away at the company's morale. Ultimately, a new normal had been established and the higher level of respect Robert's staff now had for him made him proud of how he had handled the situation.

Since then, three new projects had come in and his design teams were ahead of schedule on every one of them. That gave Robert the freedom to concentrate on the deal that was going to put his firm in a higher league, the office complex for Gibson Investments. He had e-mailed Nancy the information on the contractor he had chosen and had asked her to draw up the contract in the morning. As soon as he and Oltheim Construction signed an agreement, he would contact David to update him on his progress. Now all he had to do was think about how he was going to tell David that Cedar Rock was off limits.

Robert had not responded to David's e-mail yet. Normally, he preferred to handle this sort of situation in person. The give-and-take of a negotiation was easier when you could read the other guy's body language. But this time, there would not be any give-and-take. The estate was off the table, and Robert had to make sure David understood the decision was carved in stone. Otherwise, a powerhouse like Gibson Investments would make his life a living hell if they decided applying more pressure would convince him to sell.

Beauty puffed out a heavy whimper and her warm breath rushed up his arm. She was asleep between his legs with her head on his thigh. He stroked the fur on her neck and pushed out a heavy sigh himself. It had been a very long day for both of them.

Since Jeremy had left the manor this morning the constant flow of souls who appeared on the shore of the lake had intensified. Robert guessed it was because his attention was no longer focused on a singular soul, and so far, they were all still making their own way through purgatory. No one seemed to need him, although, he still needed the journal. Every word he had heard had stuck in his memory like glue until the soul's name was recorded on the pages of the diary. That was something that was going to take him a while to get used to, or maybe he could just have a mug of raspberry schnapps every day for breakfast.

Most of the souls who had come through Repose had acknowledged his presence and had paid their respects to the master of the manor with a gentle bow of their head, but only a few had sought out a conversation with him. The exchanges were very brief and many of them had received their heavenly joy in much the same manner as Jeremy had. Fortunately for Robert, no one else had assaulted him with the intense emotion.

The remaining souls had kept to themselves for the most part, but he had still heard their conversations. Some had spoken to themselves, and some had spoken to the souls who had come through with them. Either way, they had eventually talked through their challenges and discovered the answers they had sought.

Robert had learned that the journey through purgatory was unique to each soul. Some were limited in their senses like Jeremy, and some were able to still see the mortal world clearly. It all seemed to depend on the task they had to complete, and it didn't take long before he had learned to let them speak first while he just smiled and listened. Otherwise, they tended to expect him to come up with the answers they needed in order to move on.

After a long morning of interacting with the quests on Cedar Rock Mountain, he had decided a spectator's point of view would give him a better way to learn how the whole process worked. That was when he and Beauty had retired to the porch glider to enjoy an afternoon of soul watching before they had come inside for dinner and a nightcap.

The kindling crackled in the fireplace and a fleeting fragrance of raspberries rushed past his senses. He smiled. This house always made him feel at home. It was like being in the presence of a love that never failed. The spirit of DeLancey Manor loved him beyond his faults. He knew that more than he knew his own name, and he also knew that that love would never fade.

The scent of raspberries intensified and the figurine on the mantle caught his eye. Large wings framed the shoulders of a tall and slender man as he leaned his elbow on the mantle clock. Nathaniel was here.

Beauty opened her eyes and wagged the end of her tail, and the angel emerged from the hallway with a handful of fresh raspberries. He sat in the wing backed chair on the other side of the coffee table and tossed one into his mouth.

"This is the best part of Cedar Rock," Nathaniel said.

"Yes, it is. I noticed they never go bad either."

"You're welcome." He grinned.

Robert smiled. "You made them immortal?"

"Not me. But it was made so at my request. It was a gift for serving the Lord well." He tossed another berry into his mouth. "Have you had any today?"

"As a matter of fact, I have. They are addictive."

"That is because your body craves them. They will keep you healthy if you eat them every day." He tossed a few more into his mouth. "Look for Eleanor's recipe box. There are dozens of ways to enjoy these heavenly delectables."

"Yeah, that won't be necessary. She left it in the middle of the table. It has recipes from all the guardians." Robert folded his arms. "I took the hint that I needed to use them."

"You are a very quick study, Master Robert. They will also come in handy when you need a favor from me." Nathaniel raised an eyebrow. "Did she leave you the recipe for Shamus' raspberry schnapps?"

"Yes, and I have already had my first lesson on distilling spirits."

"Perfect! You should make a kettle of schnapps and a batch of Molly's raspberry crumb cakes."

"Well the schnapps has already been taken care of." He lifted his glass to the angel. "But schnapps and pastries together?"

"Of course. The combination is absolutely sinful. It could corrupt Gabriel."

"Angel's eat mortal food?"

"Technically, the raspberries are immortal. But a few of us do eat mortal food."

"Really?"

"Yes, but you need only worry about me. The others do not come to this mountain." He tossed the last of the berries into his mouth. "And since eating a balanced diet is not required to sustain my life, I recommend you stick to raspberries."

"That's easy enough." Robert sat up straight when Beauty jumped down to greet Nathaniel. "I'm curious though, if you don't have to eat, why do you?"

"A soul has to get his jollies somehow, and living alone on this mountain has seriously limited my options."

Robert laughed. "I suppose you're right. But if you don't mind me asking, where does the food go?"

Nathaniel slapped his hands to his stomach. "Right here."

"So, your body digests it just like mine does?"

"No. My body is made to look like yours, but it is sustained by the Holy Spirit. The food and drink I consume is absorbed by my immortal flesh." Nathaniel winked. "It is a wonder I do not have a reddish glow to my existence."

"Thank God for small favors, right?" Robert grinned.

"Something like that." Nathaniel turned his hand up and a pile of berries materialized in his palm before he popped another one into his mouth.

"So, you said if I need a favor from you, I just have to whip up a batch of schnapps and crumb cakes."

"Well, I cannot require it of you, Master Robert. But it certainly enhances my enthusiasm."

Robert hesitated. "And how many bottles of schnapps do I owe you for this morning?"

"Are you referring to that little jolt of ecstasy Jeremy gave you?"

"Yes." He couldn't help but smile. Despite the physical pain, he was looking forward to feeling the emotion again.

"You owe me nothing for that." He sighed. "It never should have happened. I was too complacent in my responsibilities."

"I thought it was an accident."

"It was. But that does not excuse my duty to protect you."

"Protect me from what? It was just a whole lot of joy."

"Master Robert, that was eternal joy, the joy of Heaven. Mortals are not capable of surviving it."

Robert rubbed his chest where he had felt his heart being crushed. The pain had been greater than anything he had ever experienced. But despite that, the joy had consumed him entirely, and the pain had become irrelevant to him.

"The pain was intense," Robert said. "I would imagine if you hadn't been there, it would have killed me eventually."

"If you had been anyone else, your mortal flesh would have died instantly." He cocked an eyebrow. "Have you not read Exodus?"

Robert suddenly felt unworthy to be in the presence of Nathaniel. He could not remember the last time he even opened a Bible let alone read one.

Sadness crept into his chest and he wished he had never brought the subject up.

"Forgive me, Master Robert." Nathaniel leaned forward, rested his elbows on his knees, and smiled. "My intention was not to shame you. I sometimes forget the word of God can be difficult for mortals to understand. I only wanted to remind you of the words that I am sure you have heard, perhaps as long ago as your childhood."

"What words are those?"

"Exodus 33:20. But, He said, you cannot see My face, for man shall not see Me and live."

"Are you saying Jeremy saw the face of God?"

"Yes. That was the joy of seeing His face."

"Then how am I still alive?"

"For one thing, it was not you who saw Him." Nathaniel leaned against the winged back of the chair and shrugged. "And, of course, being who you are and where you are had a little something to do with it."

"What are you saying? Am I...?"

"No. You are not immortal. However, you are the master of the manor, the caretaker of Purgatory, so to speak. The Holy Spirit would not choose you for this task and leave you unprotected."

"That's good to know."

"Never doubt your protection, Master Robert. You are firmly in Heaven's grasp." He grinned. "But that being said, you are still a mortal. So you will still need to use Molly's recipe for her crumb cakes."

"I will remember that."

Robert pictured Molly when she first came through the portal. She was pure feminine beauty, and she had captured his undivided attention the instant he had seen her. He was confident he had been able to regain his senses quickly enough to conceal his weakness as a mortal man, but the sting of humiliation from his inability to resist her charm was still there. He exhaled a heavy breath and leaned forward onto his elbows.

"You know," Robert said. "I have tried to imagine what the guardians were like when they were in my shoes. I can see Eleanor, Kathryn, and Shamus doing what I am doing. They are all strong in their own way. But Molly?" He paused. "She seems so soft and, well, delicate. I just can't see her doing some of this."

"Believe it or not, she was the strongest of them all."

"Really? She comes across as a socialite. I think of her as never having to lift a finger to do anything."

"Everyone makes that assumption because she uses her gift to perfection."

"Her gift?"

"She is the coyest creature I have ever seen. Her charm is otherworldly." He winked. "And I am sure she cast a bit of a spell over you when you first met her."

Robert looked at the fire in the hearth. "I suppose one of the guardians told you what happened." He paused. "I had hoped no one had noticed."

"They didn't," Nathaniel said. "I was guessing."

Robert stifled his curse and dropped his gaze to the floor.

"You are ashamed of your reaction to her?" Nathaniel said.

"Are you kidding?" Robert looked at him. "Of course, I am. I got turned on by a ghost."

"Mortal or immortal, she is a beautiful woman. You see her no differently than you see any mortal woman. She is real to you. Why is this a problem?"

"Because I know she isn't real. I mean I know she is a spirit and I still got..."

"For Heaven's sake. You are a mortal man who functions as God intended you to. There is nothing to be ashamed of." He paused. "However, I can see this is difficult for you to accept, so rest assured this information will remain between the two of us."

"Thank you," Robert said. "But I doubt it's the secret I wish it was."

"Then you are fortunate." Nathaniel smiled. "Molly will appreciate your fondness for her and she will return the favor. She is a good friend to have on your side."

"A friend. Yes, that's good."

Robert didn't hide his sigh of relief. Molly was the type of woman who could make a man thrust a sword into his own heart and smile while he did it. Thank God Shamus had promised to keep her away from him until he got a better feel for this master thing.

"By the way," Robert said, desperate to change the subject, "how is Jeremy?"

"Quite good, actually. The Lord always knows best, and despite Jeremy's complete lack of experience, he has done an amazing job protecting his son."

"What is he protecting his son from?"

"The cruelties of the mortal world." Nathaniel's expression sobered. "Guilt has destroyed Genevieve's sanity and she confessed her sin to the mortal authorities. She was convicted of murder and spent the remainder of her pregnancy in a prison infirmary. She gave birth to David and released him for adoption."

"Who adopted him?"

"No one yet. He is still a ward of the state. But all that God's will has in store for him will come to pass." Nathaniel smiled. "Jeremy will lead him to paradise."

Epilogue

The Storm

Robert sipped his schnapps and listened while Nathaniel told him stories about some of the souls he has escorted to Heaven's Gate. Most of the accounts were simple and peaceful, like his time with the late Mrs. Devonshire, who had passed through the estate the day Gracie had shown up with her basket of goodies. But a few were quite colorful, and if Robert was getting the right impression, those were the ones Nathaniel truly enjoyed escorting to paradise.

He held his glass to his lips and waited for Nathaniel to finish Miss Olga's story before he drew in the raspberry spirit. The last recount had taught him the wisdom of waiting for the finish. Just as he suspected, laughter burst forward and he had to set his glass on the coffee table in front of him.

As he regained his composure, a small lavender cloud swirled around the figurine on the mantle. When it cleared, the image of Molly stood in a stunningly demure pose. The beautiful guardian emerged from the kitchen holding a small plate of crumb cakes and another bottle of schnapps.

Robert's breath caught in his throat, and he coughed once to get it moving again. He sat up straight and smoothed out his trousers as he shifted in his seat. Hopefully he looked like the master of the manor, instead of the slovenly couch potato he felt like.

Molly moved closer and he shifted again trying to decide which pose was more professional looking. Beauty trotted past him on her way toward the food, and swatted his face with her tale. The slap was just what he needed to stop his spiral into total humiliation, and he struggled to bring a smile to his face.

He sighed. The only other woman who could turn him into a stupefied moron was a sixteen-year-old Gracie, and that was only because he was a seventeen-year-old collection of raging hormones. He was a thirty-four-year-old man now. Surely, he could keep his composure intact long enough to have an intelligent conversation with a woman who has been dead for more than sixty years.

He looked at Nathaniel who was sitting across from him, and the angel of death was grinning from ear to ear. Son of a... Nathaniel knew she was coming, and conveniently forgot to tell him.

"I thought you gentlemen would enjoy a treat while we wait," she said.

Beauty followed the plate to the coffee table. When she whimpered Molly fed her one.

"Of course, I made one for you, my dear lady." Molly caressed her head when the wolf licked its lips. "How could I not?"

Robert sat up straight and accepted the cake Molly served him.

"Thank you, Molly." Robert put his plate on the coffee table and took a big swallow from the glass of schnapps in his hand. "What did you mean when you said, 'while we wait'?"

"You did not tell him?" Molly said to Nathaniel.

"I was getting to it." Nathaniel stuffed an entire crumb cake into his mouth and waived his hand for Molly to continue while he poured himself a drink.

"Oh, for Heaven's sake." Molly sat gracefully next to Robert. "We are waiting for the soul in Repose. She is having difficulty accepting her judgement."

Robert swallowed the bite of crumb cake in his mouth. "What does that mean?"

"It means she has refused to leave the mortal world," Nathaniel said.

"Refused?" Robert said. "I didn't think you got a choice in the matter."

"Anyone can refuse paradise," Nathaniel said. "You just have to be completely daft in order to do so."

"Nathaniel," Molly said, "her situation is different than the others who have come through here and you know it."

"Different?" Robert said. "I thought Malachi took care of those ones."

"Oh no, Master Robert," Molly said. "It is nothing like that. She is to be in paradise this very moment. But her heart is stuck in the mortal world."

"What?"

"Part of her purpose in life was to test her daughter's faith in the Lord," Nathaniel said. "Now that her daughter is failing her test, she feels her sins have made her unworthy of Heaven." He scowled. "Or so she professes."

"I can only imagine her torment," Molly said.

"That doesn't make sense," Robert said. "If she has been accepted into Heaven, why is she in torment?"

"My dear man," she said, "she is grieving for her daughter. A mother only wants what is best for her children. So to stand before our Lord and discover that you were the creator of your own child's cross, and that this cross has turned her from God, would be an incredible sorrow."

"Yes, that would be an incredible sorrow if it were true," Nathaniel said. "But that is not what is holding her back."

"Of course, it is," Molly said.

"It is not. She knows her purpose in life was preordained, and that it was all necessary to prepare her for her eternal destiny."

"And you, Nathaniel, still have not grasped the depth of a mother's heart," she said. "The bond between a woman and her child is so strong it is beyond explanation, and obviously too complicated for a man to understand. Even a man as wise as you."

"I do not need to be a woman to understand one, nor do I need to be a woman to recognize a lie when one of you spews it," he said. "Lucia is hiding behind her transgressions to avoid her responsibility in Heaven."

"That is ridiculous. She is struggling with leaving her lost child behind."

"You are wrong, Molly."

"I was never wrong when it came down to helping a woman accept her destiny."

"This time," Nathaniel said, "you are."

"I am not. She is haunted by her sins."

"Listen to me. Any soul who has repented for their sins before their death and received our Lord's forgiveness, yet still claims those sins as their own, is a liar. Upon death of their mortal flesh, every soul is given the undeniable knowledge that for more than two millennia all of mankind's sins have been paid for, including their own." He stood and looked down at Molly. "Lucia is free to enter the Kingdom of Heaven and take her rightful place. But she claims a nonexistent responsibility for another soul's free will, and therefore, has turned from our Lord and arrogantly rejected the honor which has been bestowed upon her."

Molly stood, straightened her spine, and matched Nathaniel's posturing. Despite her ever present, purely feminine perfection, dominance radiated from her spirit. No doubt this was the side of Molly Nathaniel had spoken about earlier.

Her opposition to Nathaniel took Robert by surprise. He had assumed the angel of death was a higher power than the guardians. But in this moment, Molly had no intention of yielding to his authority.

"The point is," she said, "Lucia now also knows Mia has blamed our Lord for her mother's sins and has lost her faith."

"What a surprise. One soul blames The Almighty for another soul's poor choices." He paced to the hearth and gazed into the fire. "She is not the first, and disgracefully so, will not be the last."

"The limitations of mortal reasoning are to blame," she said.

"Lucia Moretti is no longer mortal," Nathaniel said. "She has been given the proper understanding and she still refuses Paradise."

"But her child's soul is at risk because of her sins," she said.

"No!" Nathaniel waved his hand across the hearth and the flames extinguished before he turned to Molly. "Mia's soul is at risk because she chooses to place the blame for sins committed against her where it does not belong."

"Mia believes her prayers went unheard. Therefore, she feels Heaven spited her because she was not rescued from an angry and meanspirited mother." Molly raised her eyebrows. "Her mother, who was a mere mortal only moments ago, can see the path of her daughter's logic. Surely the angel of death, with his superior immortal wisdom, can see it."

"That is lunacy, not logic."

"It is mortal logic."

"Then it is Mia's affair, not her mother's." Nathaniel took one step toward her. "We all have freewill, including Mia. Lucia had no more power over her daughter than you or I had, and she knows it."

"Nathaniel, please try to understand this." She blinked slowly and exhaled. "For Mia's entire childhood Lucia neglected her need for a nurturing mother and belittled her every accomplishment." She stepped close to the angel. "By the time she realized her sin the damage had been done. Mia had already turned from God."

"Like I said, that is Mia's affair, not Lucia's."

"You are stubbornness incarnate," she whispered.

Nathaniel threw her a glare of disgust and the room fell silent as he paced to the front window.

The strong wills of Nathaniel and Molly flowed from their immortal spirits. The air had gotten thick with tension and the living room was no longer a comfortable space. It felt more like a tiny linen closet. Robert took a step back to escape the smothering atmosphere and realized he had backed out of the room.

He exhaled with a grunt. This was not getting them anywhere. Neither one was going to concede their point and he'd had enough of being pushed out of his living room. It was time to move past the bickering. He stiffened his spine and forced his way through the haze of holy indignation.

"Have either of you spoken to her?" he said.

"No," Nathaniel said. "Her soul went straight to Repose when her heart stopped."

"Then how do you know she has refused her destiny?" he said

"I am kept in the loop with every soul I am entrusted to escort."

"What does that mean?"

"I can see and hear her trial." Nathaniel turned to Robert and crossed his arms. "Right now, she is pleading with Gabriel for more time."

"Exactly," Molly said. "She is desperate to save her child."

"No," Nathaniel said. "She is trying to avoid her destiny."

"Why can't you-"

"Excuse me, Molly," Robert said. "But, before Lucia gets here, I would like to make sure I understand exactly what is at stake for her." He turned to Nathaniel. "Regardless of the reason, what happens if we cannot convince her to accept her place in Heaven?"

"Her soul would be cast into Hell!"

A sudden silence filled the room and Robert felt the angel's words graze his chest like a soldier's rapier. His heart flinched, and Molly moved to his side.

"Master Robert will convince her to let go of Mia," she said to Nathaniel.

"How much time do we have?" Robert looked at her.

"That depends on Lucia," she said.

"What do you mean?" he said.

"The decision is hers to make. We retain our free will in this world. No one can make this decision for her." Molly frowned. "And the longer she waits to accept her place in Heaven, the more vulnerable she will become to Satan's deceptions. When her strength to resist is gone, her soul will be lost."

Robert had not seen Hell nor had it been described to him in any sort of detail, but somehow, he could feel the horridness of being trapped there. Maybe it was because he had experienced a piece of Heaven with a joy so intense it was incomprehensible, and if Hell was the opposite of Heaven, there should be no doubt it must be an unbearable place. His gut tightened and he rubbed the muscles to ease the discomfort. He feared this task with every cell in his body. He had to help a soul avoid eternal damnation.

"They are preparing her to leave Repose." Nathaniel unfurled his wings and a gaping hole appeared in the house above him as he turned his head toward them. "The Lord suffers greatly when a soul is lost. Remember that, always."

The moonlight reflected tiny sparks of pure white off the feathers of his wings when the evening breeze moved through them. He leapt into the air and disappeared into the dark sky. The house above them reappeared and Robert caught a glimpse of Nathaniel's wings through the front window as he flew across the water.

"What did he mean by that?" Robert looked at Molly.

"When a soul rejects Paradise, it rejects the Lord. Every soul who rejects the Lord causes Him great despair."

"Because He loves us," Robert said.

"Yes," she said.

"Then there is no time to waste."

Molly smiled and Beauty trotted to the front door. Robert crossed the threshold before them and saw an older woman standing at the base of the porch stairs. Her face was aged with subtle lines around her mouth and eyes, and sorrow was heavy in her gaze.

"Master Robert," she said. "I was told you could help me."

ABOUT THE AUTHOR

Susan Baer received her Bachelor of Fine Arts degree from Edinboro University of Pennsylvania in 1990. Her three-dimensional works of art were made from clay, stone, and precious and semi-precious metals. Despite her original plan to build a career as an artist, she donated most of her pieces and never sold them commercially.

In 2001, she began writing short stories and scenes for romance and spiritually based paranormal fiction. She self-published the first of her romance novels in 2015 and completed the five-book series in 2017. Although her previously published works were written in a secular genre, she has returned to her original love of spiritual fiction. She draws her inspiration from her devote Catholic upbringing and expresses her love of God through her stories. Unfaithful is the second book in a series of tales about how the all loving, benevolent Creator leads all souls to Heaven.

Other Titles by Susan M. Baer

The Master of DeLancey Manor, *Cedar Rock Mountain, Book I*

Find out more about Susan M. Baer and her

upcoming books online at

www.susanbaerauthor.com